Hansel and Gretel

and other stories

Miles
KeLLy

First published in 2011 by Miles Kelly Publishing Ltd
Harding's Barn, Bardfield End Green, Thaxted, Essex, CM6 3PX, UK

2 4 6 8 10 9 7 5 3 1

Publishing Director Belinda Gallagher

Creative Director Jo Cowan

Editor Amanda Askew

Senior Designer Joe Jones

Designer Kayleigh Allen

Production Manager Elizabeth Collins

Reprographics Anthony Cambray, Stephan Davis, Jennifer Hunt

ISBN 978-1-84810-440-2

Printed in China

British Library Cataloguing-in-Publication Data
A catalogue record for this book is available from the British Library

ACKNOWLEDGEMENTS
Artworks are from the Miles Kelly Artwork Bank

Made with paper from a sustainable forest

www.mileskelly.net
info@mileskelly.net

www.factsforprojects.com

Self-publish your
children's book

buddingpress.co.uk

Contents

Peter and the Wolf 4

The Selfish Giant 8

The Red Shoes 15

Cap o' Rushes 22

The Sorcerer's Apprentice 28

Hansel and Gretel 33

Peter and the Wolf

Original libretto by Sergei Prokofiev

Peter lived with his grandfather at the edge of the forest. Peter used to play with the wild birds and animals in the garden, but his grandfather always warned him not to go into the meadow in case the wolf crept out of the forest.

I am afraid Peter did not always do as he was told, so one day he slipped through the garden gate and into the meadow when he met a duck swimming in the middle of the pond.

"You must watch out for the wolf," said Peter to the duck but she was busy enjoying herself and did not listen. A little bird flew down and the duck tried to persuade her to come into the pond as well. But as the little bird stood talking to the duck, Peter saw the cat sneak up behind her.

"Look out!" shouted Peter and the bird flew up to safety in the tree.

"Thank you, Peter," she said. The cat was not so pleased. Just then Peter's grandfather came out and saw the open garden gate.

"Peter! How many times do I have to tell you? Come back into the garden at once," he shouted and Peter walked slowly back in.

Meanwhile, at the far side of the meadow, near the forest, a grey shape slunk from under the trees. It was the wolf! The little bird flew up into the tree, and the cat joined her – but on a lower branch.

But the duck was too busy swimming to see what was happening and in a flash the wolf grabbed her and swallowed her whole!

Peter saw it all from the garden. "I am going to catch that old wolf," he said to himself.

He found a piece of rope and climbed up a tree whose branches overhung the meadow. He made a loop in the rope and hung it out of the tree. Then he called to the little bird, "Can you tempt the wolf this way by flying round his head, please? I am going to catch him!"

The brave little bird darted down very close to the wolf's nose. The wolf snapped his fierce teeth, and only just missed the little bird. Closer and closer they came to the tree where Peter was hiding. The wolf was so busy trying to catch the bird that he did not see the rope. Peter looped it over the wolf's tail, and there he was, dangling from the branch of the tree!

Peter's grandfather came out and he was astonished to see the wolf. Then some hunters came out of the forest.

"Well done," they cried, "you have caught the wolf. We have been after him for a long time."

And they all went off in a joyful procession to the zoo. Peter led the wolf at the front, the little bird flew overhead, and the cat padded alongside. The hunters came up in the rear with Peter's grandfather. And from inside the wolf's tummy, the duck quacked loudly, just to remind everyone that she was there!

The Selfish Giant

By Oscar Wilde

Once there was a beautiful garden in which the children used to play every day on their way home from school. The children didn't think that the beautiful garden belonged to anyone in particular. But one day a huge giant strode in and boomed, "What are you all doing here? This is MY garden. Get lost!" Seven years ago, the giant had gone to visit his friend the Cornish ogre. Now he was back and he wanted his garden all to himself.

Of course, the children ran away at once. But the giant wasn't satisfied. He put up a high fence all the way around his garden with a noticeboard outside which read 'TRESPASSERS WILL BE PROSECUTED'. He really was a very selfish giant.

Now the poor children had nowhere to play. But the giant didn't give any thought to that. He was too busy wondering why the blossom had fallen from the trees, why the flowers had withered, and why all the birds had flown away. Surely it is meant to be the springtime, the giant thought to himself as he looked out of the window and saw huge flakes of snow tumbling from the sky. Frost painted the trees silver. A blanket of ice chilled the ground and hardened the plants into stiff, lifeless spikes. Day after day, the north wind roared around the giant's garden, zooming around his roof and howling down his chimney pots. And the hail came too, battering on the giant's windows until he bellowed with annoyance and clapped his hands over his ears against the noisy rattling.

Then one Saturday, the giant woke to a sound he had almost forgotten – it was a bird, chirruping in his garden. A beautiful perfume tickled the giant's nose… the scent of flowers! "Spring has come at last!" the giant beamed, and he pulled on his clothes and ran out into his garden.

The giant couldn't believe what he saw. The snow had melted, the frost was gone, the sky was blue and the breeze was gentle. And there were children everywhere. They had crept back into his garden through a hole that had worn away in the fence. Now children were sitting in trees heavy with ripe fruit. Playing among flowerbeds filled with nodding blossoms. Running over emerald green grass scattered with daisies and buttercups. And the sound of their happy laughter filled the air.

Only in one corner of the garden was it still winter. A little boy was standing in a patch of snow, looking up at the bare branches of a chestnut tree and crying because he couldn't reach it.

The giant's heart ached as he watched. "Now I know what makes my garden beautiful," he said. "It is the children. How selfish I have been!"

The giant strode through the garden towards the sobbing little boy. He scooped him up gently and set him among the icy boughs of the chestnut tree.

At once, leaves appeared all over the branches. It was spring. The little boy's face brightened into a huge smile and he reached his arms up around the giant's neck and hugged him.

"It is your garden now, little children," laughed the giant. The giant took his axe, knocked down the fence and had more fun than he had ever had before, playing with them all day. Only one thing spoiled the giant's new happiness. He looked all over his garden for the little boy whom he had helped into the tree, but he was nowhere to be found. The giant loved the little boy the best, because he had hugged him, and he longed more than anything to see his friend again.

Many years passed and the children came every day to play in the garden. The giant became old and creaky. Eventually he could no longer run about and let the children climb over him as he had done. He sat in a special armchair so he could watch the children enjoying themselves. "My garden is beautiful," he would say to himself, "but the children are the most beautiful things of all." Sometimes the giant's grey head would nod and he would begin to snore, and the children would creep away quietly so they didn't disturb him.

One afternoon, the giant woke from a little doze to see an astonishing sight. In the far corner of his garden was a golden tree he had never seen before. The giant's heart leapt for joy, for standing underneath it was the boy he had loved.

The giant heaved himself up from his armchair and shuffled across the grass as fast as his old legs would take him. But when he drew near the boy, his face grew black as thunder – there were wounds on the little boy's palms and on his feet. "Who has dared to hurt you?" boomed the giant. "Tell me, and I will go after them with my big axe!"

"These are the marks of love," the little boy smiled. He took the giant's hand. "Once, you let me play in your garden," he said. "And today, you shall come with me to mine, which is in Paradise."

And when the children came running to play that afternoon, they found the giant lying dead under the beautiful tree, covered with a beautiful blanket of snowy-white blossoms.

The Red Shoes

By Hans Christian Andersen

There was once a woman who was so poor that she couldn't afford to buy her daughter Karen any shoes. The woman often wept to see Karen's feet all rough and blistered. She would have been overjoyed to know that the shoemaker's wife felt so sorry for Karen that she was making her a pair of red shoes from some leftover leather. But the woman never found out. She died the very day that the red shoes were finished and Karen wore them for the first time as she walked behind her mother's coffin on the way to church.

The shoemaker's wife couldn't sew very well and the shoes had turned out to be rather clumsy and misshapen. But Karen thought that her soft, red shoes were the most wonderful things in the world.

But the old lady who kindly took Karen in said, "You can't possibly go walking around in those odd things. Whatever will people think?" She threw the red shoes onto the fire and bought Karen a pair of sensible, sturdy black ones.

It was the sensible, sturdy black shoes that Karen was wearing when the old lady took her to the palace to see the parade for the little princess's birthday. The king and queen stood with the little princess on the balcony, waving and smiling. But Karen didn't look at the gracious expressions on their faces, or their fine, rich robes. Karen couldn't take her eyes off the red shoes on the feet of the princess. They were made of satin, not leather, so they shone like rubies. Those really are the most wonderful things in all the world, thought Karen.

From that moment, whenever Karen buckled on her sensible, black shoes, she thought of the little princess's beautiful red ones. Whenever Karen took off her sensible, black shoes, she thought of the princess's beautiful red ones. And she longed for those beautiful red shoes with all her heart.

One day, the old lady who looked after Karen

looked at her sensible, black shoes and tutted,
"My, my! Those are looking rather old and shabby
– and they're too small for you now. We can't
have you going along to church in those
tomorrow." The old lady handed her a purse full of
money. "Buy yourself some new ones," she smiled.

Karen walked all the way to the shoe shop with
a thumping heart. First, she tried on some
sensible, sturdy black shoes – but none fit her.
Then she tried on some smart, lace-up brown
shoes – but they either slopped up and down or
cramped her toes. Then Karen peered up at a high
shelf and saw a red pair exactly like the ones the
little princess had worn. They fitted her perfectly.
Karen held her breath as she handed over her
money and stepped out of the shop. Her feet
gleamed and twinkled in the sunlight. She could
hardly believe it. Her dream had come true.

Karen knew full well that the old lady wouldn't approve at all of her choice. But luckily for her, the old lady's eyesight wasn't what it was, and the colour of Karen's new shoes was just a dark blur. Karen kept quiet, saying nothing of the truth.

Next day, Karen's heart nearly burst with excitement as she slipped on her shoes. She tripped gaily to church, and even though there were many finely dressed people about, she had eyes for no one and nothing except the red shoes. She hoped that everyone would see them.

Even as Karen sat in her church pew, she couldn't take her eyes off her red shoes.

Even when the priest was praying, she couldn't take her eyes off her red shoes. Even when the organist began to strike up a hymn of praise, she couldn't take her eyes off her red shoes. The statues of the angels and saints seemed to frown down sternly upon her, but Karen didn't notice. She still couldn't take her eyes off the red shoes.

As the choir started to sing and their voices filled the air, Karen felt a strange sensation in her feet. Her toes began to twitch inside the red satin. Her heels began to quiver. Suddenly, Karen's feet began to dance. Right there and then in church, her red shoes forced her to stand up and leap and turn and skip. With the eyes of everyone upon her, the red shoes danced her down the aisle and out into the sunlight. "Help me!" she cried, but no one knew what to do. The red shoes danced Karen all around the graveyard and out of the church gate.

Then they danced her round and round the churchyard wall and off down the street...

By day and by night, the enchanted red shoes carried Karen along, twinkling wickedly. They danced her in and out of houses and up and down stairs. They danced her through the city gates, across the fields and into the dark forest. They danced her out of the trees and through meadows, until Karen had forgotten how long she had been dancing... and still they made her dance. "Forgive me!" the sobbing girl cried out. "Forgive me for thinking of these foolish things above everything else!" At last, the red shoes were still. Utterly exhausted, Karen collapsed into a heap and closed her eyes. And when her soul reached heaven, she never had to dance or think about red shoes ever again.

Cap o' Rushes

By Joseph Jacobs

There was once a rich gentleman who had three daughters. He thought he'd see how fond they were of him, so he said to the first, "How much do you love me?"

"Why," said she, "as I love my life."

He said to the next, "How much do you love me?"

"Why," said she, "better than all the world."

He said to the last, "How much do you love me?"

"I love you as fresh meat loves salt," said she.

Her father was angry. "You don't love me," said he, "and in my house you will stay no more." And he drove her out there and then.

She went away till she came to a fen. She made some rushes into a cloak with a hood, to hide her fine clothes. Then she came to a great house.

"Do you want a maid?" said she. "I ask no wages, and do any sort of work."

"Well," said they, "if you would like to wash the pots and scrape the saucepans you may stay."

So she stayed and did all the dirty work. She gave no name so they called her 'Cap o' Rushes'.

One day there was to be a dance a little way off. The servants were allowed to go, but Cap o' Rushes said she was too tired. But when the others had left, she took off her cap and went to the dance.

Well, who should be there but her master's son, and what should he do but fall in love with her?

He would dance with no one else.

Next morning the other maids said, "You missed a sight, Cap o' Rushes! The most beautiful lady you ever saw, dressed so grand. The master never took his eyes off her."

"I should have liked to have seen her," she replied.

"There's another dance this evening. Perhaps she'll come."

But in the evening, Cap o' Rushes said she was too tired to go.

When they were gone, she took off her cap and went to the dance. The master's son danced with no one else, and never took his eyes off her.

Next day the other maids said again, "Cap o' Rushes, you should ha' been there to see the lady. There she was, gay and grand. There's a dance again tonight. You must go with us."

Well, come that evening, Cap o' Rushes said she was too tired to go, and do what they would she stayed at home. But when they were gone, she took off her cap and went to the dance.

The master's son gave her a ring and told her if he didn't see her again he should die. But before the dance was over, she slipped away again.

The next day, the master's son tried to find out where the lady had gone, but no one knew. He got worse for the love of her till he had to stay in bed.

"Make some gruel for the master," they said to the cook. The cook set about making it when Cap o' Rushes came in.

"What are you doing?" said she.

"I'm going to make some gruel for the master," said the cook, "for he's dying for love of the lady."

"Let me make it," said Cap o' Rushes.

Cap o' Rushes made the gruel, and slipped the ring into it before the cook took it upstairs.

The young man drank it and saw the ring at the bottom. "Who made this gruel here?" said he.

"'Twas Cap o' Rushes," said the cook.

"Send Cap o' Rushes here," said he.

So Cap o' Rushes came.

"Did you make my gruel?" said he.

"Yes, I did," said she.

"Where did you get this ring?" said he.

"From him that gave it me," said she.

"Who are you, then?" said the young man.

"I'll show you," said she. She took off her cap o' rushes, and there she was in her beautiful clothes.

They married soon after and everyone was

asked to the wedding – even Cap o' Rushes' father. But she never said who she was.

Before the wedding, she asked the cook to dress every dish without a grain of salt.

"That'll be nasty," said the cook.

"That doesn't matter," said she.

The wedding day came, and they were married, and everyone sat down to dinner. The meat was so tasteless they couldn't eat it. Cap o' Rushes' father burst out crying.

"What is the matter?" asked the master's son.

"I had a daughter," said he, "and I asked her how much she loved me. She said, 'As much as fresh meat loves salt.' I turned her from my door, thinking she didn't love me. Now I see she loved me best of all. She may be dead for all I know."

"No, father, I am here!" Cap o' Rushes put her arms round him. They were all happy ever after.

The Sorcerer's Apprentice

A German folk tale

The sorcerer lived in a dusty room at the top of a tall gloomy tower. His table was covered with bottles and jars full of strange-coloured potions, and bubbling mixtures filled the air with horrible smells. The walls of the tower were lined with huge old books. These were the sorcerer's spell books and he would let no one else look inside them.

The sorcerer had a young apprentice called Harry – a good but lazy boy who longed to do magic himself. The sorcerer had promised to teach him, but only when Harry was ready.

One day the sorcerer had to visit a friend. He had never left Harry alone in the tower before and he did not entirely trust him. Looking fierce, the sorcerer gave Harry his instructions.

"I have an important spell to conjure up when I return. I need the cauldron full of water from the well," he said. "When you have filled the cauldron, you can sweep the floor and light the fire."

Harry was not pleased. It would take many trips to the well to fill the cauldron, and he would have many steps to climb each time. The sorcerer climbed onto his small green dragon and said, "Touch nothing!" before flying off in a cloud of smoke and flame from the dragon.

Harry watched until the sorcerer was safely out of sight. Then he took one of the spell books and turned the pages until he found what he was looking for – a spell to make a broomstick obey orders. He read the spell out loud.

The broomstick quivered and then stood up. It grabbed a bucket and jumped off down the stairs. Soon it was back, the bucket full of water. It tipped the water into the cauldron and set off down the stairs again. Harry was delighted. On and on the broomstick went and the cauldron soon was full.

"Stop, stop!" shouted Harry, but

the broomstick just carried on, and on. Soon the floor was awash and bottles and jars were floating around the room. Nothing Harry could say would stop the broomstick. In desperation, he grabbed the axe that lay by the fireside and chopped the broomstick into bits. To his horror, all the pieces turned into new broomsticks and set off to the well, buckets appearing magically in their hands.

By now the water was nearly up to the ceiling

and Harry
gave himself up
for lost. Suddenly
there was a clatter of
wings and a hiss of steam
as the dragon flew into the
tower. The sorcerer was back!
He ordered the broomsticks to stop.
They did. Then he ordered the water back into the
well. It all rushed back down the stairs. Then he
ordered the dragon to dry everything with its hot
breath. Then he turned to look at Harry. Harry
could see that the sorcerer was very angry. The
sorcerer looked as if he might turn Harry into a
frog, but then he sat down on a soggy cushion.

"Right, I think it is time I taught you how to do
magic PROPERLY!" And he did.

Hansel and Gretel

By the Brothers Grimm

At the edge of a forest lived a poor woodcutter and his wife – a spiteful woman – and their two children, Hansel and Gretel. They were very poor so there was often very little food on the table.

One day there was no food at all. Everyone went to bed hungry. That night, Hansel heard his mother tell his father, "Husband, there are too many mouths to feed. You must leave the children in the forest tomorrow."

"Wife, I cannot abandon our children, there are wolves in the forest!" said the poor woodcutter.

But his wife made him agree to her evil plan. Hansel felt his heart grow icy cold. But he was a clever boy and so he slipped out of the house and filled his pockets with shiny white stones.

The next morning they all rose early and the children followed their father deep into the forest.

He lit them a fire and told them he was going to gather wood and would be back to collect them. He left them, tears falling down his face.

The day passed slowly. Hansel kept their fire going but when night fell, it grew very cold and they could hear all kinds of rustling under the shadowy trees. Gretel could not understand why their father had not come back to collect them, so Hansel had to tell her that their mother had told the woodcutter to leave them there deliberately.

"But don't worry, Gretel," he said, "I will lead us home," and in the moonlight he showed her the line of shiny white stones that he had dropped from his pocket, one by one, as their father had led them into the forest. They were soon home where their father greeted them with great joy. But their mother was not pleased.

Some time passed. They managed to survive

with very little to eat but another day came when Hansel heard his mother demanding that the woodcutter leave them in the forest again. And when Hansel went to collect some more pebbles, he found the door locked and he couldn't get out.

In the morning, their father gave them each a piece of bread, and led them even deeper into the forest than before. All day long, Hansel comforted Gretel and told her that this time he had left a trail of breadcrumbs to lead them safely back home. But when the moon rose and the children set off there was not a breadcrumb to be seen. The birds had eaten every last one. There was nothing to do but go to sleep and wait until the morning.

The next day they walked and walked, but they saw nothing but trees. And the next day was the same. By this time they were not only cold and hungry but deeply frightened. It looked as if they would never ever be able to find a way out of the forest. But just as it was getting dark, they came to a clearing, and there stood a strange house.

The walls were made of gingerbread, the windows of fine spun sugar and the tiles on the roof were brightly striped sweets. Hansel and Gretel could not believe their luck and were soon breaking off bits of the house to eat. Then a little voice came from inside.

"Nibble, nibble, little mouse,
    Who is that eating my sweet house?"

Out of the front door came a very old woman. She smiled sweetly at the children and said, "Dear ones, you don't need to eat my house. Come inside and I will give you lots to eat and you shall sleep in warm beds." Hansel and Gretel needed no second asking. They were soon tucked up, warm and full of hot milk, ginger biscuits and apples. They both fell asleep quickly. Little did they know they were in worse danger than ever before. The old woman was a wicked witch and she had decided to make Gretel work in the kitchen, and worst of all, she planned to fatten Hansel up so she might eat him!

The very next morning she locked poor Hansel in a cage and gave Gretel a broom and told her to clean the house from top to toe. In the evening, the witch fed Hansel a huge plate of chicken but she only gave Gretel a dry hunk of bread. But once she was asleep, Hansel shared his meal with Gretel.

So they lived for many days. The witch could not see very well, so every morning she made Hansel put his finger through the cage so she could tell how fat he was getting. But clever Hansel poked a chicken bone through the bars so the witch thought he was still too skinny to eat.

After many days, she grew fed up and decided to eat him anyway. She asked Gretel to help her prepare the big oven. The witch made some bread to go with her supper and when the oven was hot, she put it in to cook. When the bread was ready the witch asked Gretel to lift it out to cool. But Gretel was clever too. She pretended she couldn't reach the tray, and when the witch bent down inside the oven Gretel gave her a great shove and closed the door. And that was the end of the witch!

Gretel released Hansel, and together they set off once more to try to find their way home. After all their adventures, fortune finally smiled on them and they soon found the path home. Their father was simply overjoyed to see them again. And what, you might ask, of their mean mother? Well, the poor woodcutter had not had a happy moment since he left the children in the forest. He had become so miserable that she decided there was no living with him. The day before Hansel and Gretel returned, she had upped sticks and left. That served her right, didn't it?